Welcome to The Magic of Old Gold Watches

By Lew Hollander

Produced in the UNITED STATES OF AMERICA
Authored by LEWIS E. HOLLANDER, JR
Designed by EAGLE LADY DESIGN STUDIO
Published by GREEN MANSIONS, INC., LEWIS E. HOLLANDER, JR
PO Box 388, Florence, OR 97439

BOOK COVER:
Photography by LEWIS E. HOLLANDER, JR AND KAREN HOLLANDER
Designed by EAGLE LADY DESIGN STUDIO

ISBN: 979-8-218-34639-3

BOOKS BY AND ABOUT LEWIS E. HOLLANDER:
And Chocolate Shall Lead Us
And Chocolate Shall Lead Us (for children)
Endurance Riding, From Beginning to Winning
Use it or Lose It, Lew Hollander's Biography

For ordering books:
Available on Amazon.com
www.LewHollander.org

Book Stores and Retail Stores:
Order wholesale directly from IngramSpark

DEDICATION

To my sister Margret Louise Crystal, died 1/16/22.

CONTENTS

The Magic of Old Gold Watches
By Lew Hollander

Your **watch** does not have to be pure gold or fancy jewels. I am interested in the time from the late seventies through the early nineteen hundreds. The subject of old gold watches is called "Horology". This is the time when men and women clutched their solid gold or gold filled watches and especially the fun, hunter **watches** that popped open, were a bright spot in the landscape of a down trodden population. Yes the rich were swinging high as they still do. But now we have cell phones and TV. At least then they did not invade our home instead of street hawkers, now they come right into our home onto the giant TV like you are supposed to have, so you can hear all the ridiculous advertisements. Does this help anything, no, does it teach you anything? No. Maybe we were better with our beautiful pocket **watch**. I just want to get you prepared for life in the late 1880s and see what comfort and joy was derived from those beautiful **pocket watches**. They were an achievement of great engineering and art combined. Those who were there felt a warm and fuzzy feeling whipping out a gold watch and stroking it. I think I am more comfortable with that idea than of a cell phone. Now finally you get to the purpose of this book and it is to get to the life surrounding the gold pocket **watches**, and the magic within them. I have eleven gold **watches**. Each watch is different and has a different story all of its own. I will try to bring back scenes from that era long past now. I guess this is

because I was born on June 6, 1930 and my parents were both born in the `19th century, so I feel connected. If you would enjoy my fantasy adventures with each **watch** then come with me. Yes I will put it in Audio for those who do not read anymore. If you have never felt a gold pocket watch, go to any pong shop and check a few out. (If you want to buy an old gold watch look on E Bay) There is a spirit there that is emanating from the **watch**, I can feel it, tells me about the former owners and those that share my feelings. They all had lives and loves and wants and desires. The method I used was to, hold each **watch** in my hand and listen to the stories that poured out through my imagination. As a scientist (physicist) I find it hard to divert from the facts. But I am going off into a new adventure with his book. These are stories that came to me from each of the eight **watches**. Lew, why did not you use the other three **watches** you have. That is a fair question. They are personal; one is my father's so that is private, two are ladies **watches**, smaller and one is my mother's and the other was given to me by a special person. The reason I have a majority of Waltham watches, is when I was little my father had a Hunter model Waltham and I thought it was so cool when he would take it out of his pocket and push the button and the gold cover would pop open to see the time. The hunter case is so exciting as it pops open. What fun, what command you have over the surrounding folks. Click, and it opens, I love that idea.

Watch #1

*Is an Elgin solid gold, serial # 13712298
and case # 1345432
it was made around 1870-1871
it was the rich man's watch.*

The Setting

I see that there was a long rambling house, white, lots of rooms and a very large yard near the Atlantic Ocean. The house had three garages and a few workshops. Who lives here? Only a very senior, military officer, old, stern and demanding obedience from everyone including his young son, called Bill. Where is the mother? The only residences were the father, the boy and several servants. There was a full time gardener, a cook, and a chauffeur. His lands were open and well kept and a lot of room to run and play. This is defiantly a rich man's home.

The gentleman is old and grouchy. No time for his young son who is full of life and is a sort of a dare devil, which irritates the old gentlemen. He would prefer a student, grade A and always on time but no Bill is always late and just gets by at school. What will happen to Bill? At the death of his father Bill inherits the watch. He will always keep the watch with him and he will move to Florida and invest in real estate and ride a motorcycle but always have the Watch with him until the day he crashes his motorcycle and he dies.

Watch #2

*Is a Waltham made in 1877, Waltham watches were the first gold watches to be made in the USA starting in 1853. There were 150 of them made. #1035944 Seven Jewel movement, it is not railroad grade. It is a hunter **watch**, pops open to read the time. Gold filled. It has a double case and a pop open hunter type **watch**. It actually has a front cover which pops open, a cover for the movement and then a third cover which snaps shut for the case.*

The Setting

The family moved from the East coast to the mid west and built a small house during the movement west. Dad was poor but always wanted a Waltham watch, the hunter model. Before they left the East he bought one, just perfect and it was the pride of his life. The family had seven children three boys and four girls. Everyone helped on the farm. They barely had enough to eat and clothing, nails, boards were expensive but it was better than city life and he still had his watch. The one luxury was the Waltham watch which, dad wore every day, and had brought with him to the farm. The land was good and the rains came and the family prospered. The girls went off to different professions and the boys stayed home and worked the farm and built their own houses. They acquired adjacent lands. All went very well and they became affluent. When dad died the oldest son got the Waltham and wore it every day. However the successor offspring were in 1930, were confronted by the drought and dust bowl. The farm was lost and the Waltham was lost. But the Waltham had served many successor families for many years.

WATCH #3

*Very interesting watch made by Tracy Watch Co. It is the AMBIRAL no date but a patent number date is 1906. This is a non Magnetic **watch** and had two serial numbers #81110635 and #1770635 maybe the movement and the case which is a Wilson case. The watch was designed for people working with high voltage, electricians, medical workers. The higher voltages caused a slight error in the time keeping of gold **watches**.*

THE SETTING

It is beautiful home, two stories, columns on the porch setting off the picture and an expansive lawn in front on a Chicago upscale boulevard. This house is owned by a doctor who works with x-rays all day. An x-ray machine needs very high voltages to accelerate the electrons against the target thus emitting x-rays. X-rays were discovered by William Roentgen in 1895 and put into service by doctors in the early 1900s. But many investigators and diagnostic clinicians died from the exposure. So our Chicago doctor had to protect his own life with lead aprons and concrete walls. He also needed to have a watch that was non-magnetic so it would not error in the high voltage fields. He would come home to a beautiful young wife and their two children, a boy and a girl. Either one of the children could not have been over 10 years old when the Doctor died of radiation overdose. This was common in those times. The boy was the oldest and he inherited the non magnetic watch which he carried where ever he went in life.

WATCH #4

A Waltham Watch,
made around 1898 and 1899,
gold filled #8816250,
with gold filigree hands and a
hunter style case that pops open.

The Setting

Is a Bar, a saloon in down town Boston. Now this was an Irish Pub complete with portly older gentlemen who gathered every evening about quarter to five. The owner, a retired Army Captain and a pioneer for the US Army Signal Corp in telegraphy and communications, drank with the best of them. He also ran up San Juan Hill in Santiago de Cuba on July 1, 1898 with Teddy Roosevelt. He was a fun loving fellow and gave all his patrons pleasant surroundings and lively discussions. He used his Waltham watch to open and to close right on time every day. That watch was one of the most accurate and beautiful Hunter watches available. One night a fight broke out and the owner was seriously injured, but he held fast to his Waltham watch and died with it in his hand. It went to one of his many obligations that you acquire being a pub owner.

WATCH #5

*A Waltham Watch
I guess was produced
about 1880 and is still running.*

The Setting

This watch was passed from Father to son many times winding up in San Francisco and being swiped up in the California gold rush which started in 1848. Our watch arrived later carried by a very bright young man years later. He looked over the prospects of prospecting in the Sierra Foothills and perceived the statistical odds on making a fortune were slim to none. He did read the large market for tools, mining equipment, food, building materials and the like. So with great reluctance he went to the pawn shop in San Francisco and hocked his precious Waltham watch. With this money he bought his first load of tools, food and sundries, a wagon and a mule. This was a very big move for him. He headed for Auburn, California without a Penny in his pocket. In an hour he had sold all his goods and was on his way back to San Fran where, with the money he made he bought two more wagons hired a driver and was off again to Auburn. He did not stop to eat or sleep but continued to buy wagons and hire drivers. At the end of the month he had over 30 wagons running. He then reclaimed his Waltham Watch bought himself a home and became one of the richest men in San Fran. He then went back to the pawn shop and bought it lock stock and barrel. From there he ran retail stores and kept expanding. The watch was never far from his side and his children cherished it, having it on the mantel piece.

Watch #6

*American Waltham Watch
Co. 17 Jewels case #8813704
movement # 19055213,
Black hands, guess it was made about 1898*

The Setting

This watch belonged to a news paper copy man in Indiana. He had been working for about ten years and was fed up with his situation. He had heard that there was a gold rush in the Klondike, Alaska. So he decided to travel to Juneau by train, boat and horse. He had saved some money and he had a Waltham gold watch which he was never without. Once in Juneau, he bought a wagon, a mule and supplies. It was a very arduous and dangerous trek to the Klondike gold fields that borders on the Canadian border. Now there is a highway. He knew little to nothing about mining but hoped to strike it rich. He interviewed the local prospectors for tips on what to do and what not to do. He would help some of the miners and learn the techniques from them. The more he moved around the gold field, the less he was driven to start a claim himself. He traveled over the Canadian border which was a big mistake. He was way laid, beaten up and his wonderful Waltham watch was stolen. Instead of digging he decided to start a local news letter which turned into a paper and did well for him. One day a Canadian Mountie came to his office and asked if he could identify a Waltham watch which the Mountie had heard was stolen from him. He had his name inscribed in the case and the Mountie had arrested a trouble maker and thief who had his watch. He was delighted and never let that watch out of his sight. Good things happen for people with gold watches.

WATCH #7

Elgin812 #22604812
about 1924 Military issue

THE SETTING

This watch was issued to Francisco a new US Army recruit and was probably an incentive to sign up. WW I ran from 1914 to 1918 so his enlistment could have been after WW I. When he was discharged from the Army he took up a profession as an artist specializing in murals on sign boards and buildings. He married a young Mexican girl that he met in Monterey, Mexico. They were a happy couple and had three children, two boys and a lovely girl. His paintings were admired everywhere. When the children grew up, the couple took to traveling around the world and hosted clinics on the art of mural painting. An Arab Sheik, from The United Arab Emirates, was so impressed with his talent that he had him paint the whole side of his place wall. It turned out to be the pride of the UAE and the rest of the Arab world. In the UAE his gold watch was envied by everyone. After returning home he built a luxurious, small home just big enough for him and his partner, confidant, confessor, friend, lover and wife to live in. The watch had stayed with him through all their travels. Now that they are settled down in their new home, tragedy struck and their new house burned to the ground along with his precious Elgin watch.

Watch #8

Hamilton Watch Co.
Started making watches in 1892
at that time the Hamilton watch was
the highest Quality watch on the market.
This watch is 1893 vintage and Gold filled.

THE SETTING

This Hamilton was owned by a kindly older gentlemen. In the old days, once a person owned a beautiful watch like this he would keep the watch his entire life. His wife had predeceased him and he was very lonely. They had no children but a beautiful relationship together until her death. Life spans were short and medical treatments were very limited. The only thing he had left was his memories and his gold watch, which she had given him.

In an entirely separate incident; there was a terrible accident where the mother and father were killed and their young son, Paul was injured. There was no one to care for him so he was delivered Paul to the orphanage which was on the same block as the owner of the Hamilton watch. Now as time passed by the boy played in the street, and then he was invited into the gentlemen's back yard. They talked and both were lonely so it turned out to be a great friendship. Paul grew into a fine young man both the older man and Paul would spend considerable time together since they enjoyed each other's company. The orphanage was quiet happy with the relationship and always knew where to find Paul. As the gentlemen grew older he decided to give his precious watch to Paul so that another generation could enjoy the magnificence of the watch. Then, years later the watch was past down to the Paul's number two son, whom he preferred over the older boy who had paid little attention to him in his older days.

CONCLUSION

The story of the old gold watches such as Waltham, Hamilton and Elgin was astounding. In 1853, when Waltham made the first gold watch in America, a new level of technology came to North America. Look at the pictures of the open cases to appreciate the tiny delicate parts and jewel set gears and the beautiful engravings to say nothing of the gold cases. The entire nation beat to the rhythm of the gold watch. Anyone who could afford, one had one. It was not only a sign status but you usually arrived at appointments on time. Keep in mind that each part, tiny gears, shims, jewels were used as bearings, very fine hands even a second hand all made by hand from metals forged in those early days. The art work on each was a masterpiece. Go to YouTube, look up old gold pocket watches and how to rebuild them from the start and see the plethora of parts required to make a watch. Think they machined those parts from steel that had to be made in a foundry and then machined to paper thin tiny parts. Those watches are still running today if they were properly maintained. This is more than can be said for computers, cell phones even modern buildings. OH the old churches are still standing and so are the castles just like the old gold watches. Once artificial Intelligence is securely in control it will be interesting to see the direction it will lead us. I hope AI includes a love for old gold watches. From Gold Watches to cell phones and computers the story goes on, I hope.

SANDCASTLES

It all began. at the beach building sandcastles with walls, dripped turrets, moats, and drainage ditches knowing that the ocean tides would come in and level them and tomorrow I would have to build again. Little did I realize that this was a pattern of life. How we build and then tear down our creations and we grow old with a legion of torn down sandcastles. A trail of wreckage left behind and like the tide we are then swept away leaving very little to remember us by.

—Thought for the day by Lew

The **Magic** of OLD GOLD WATCHES

ABOUT THE AUTHOR
Lew Hollander

**Physicist (Nanotechnology) • Author • Triathlete
World Champion, Guinness Book of Records
Endurance Rider Hall of Fame • Over 70 Ironman Completions**

Lewis E. Hollander Jr. (born June 6, 1930) is a physicist, author and Ironman World Age Group champion triathlete. He is listed in the Guinness Book of World Records for being the oldest to finish the Hawaii Ironman at 82.[1] Buy Books: Lew's Website: LewHollander.org

Finisher 2002 Hawaii Ironman 14:43:40 at Age 72 with Grand Daughter, Chantelle Shields

Lew Hollander 80 years old. 15 Hours 48 Min 39 Sec Course Record, 2010 Kona, Hawaii Ironman

ISBN: 979-8-218-34639-3
$15.00

WILLIAM BROOKS
AND
DR. GEORGE SAYRE JR.

ON THE
WAY